From

Amy's Angel

for Robin Patterson

Published in Nashville, Tennessee, by Thomas Nelson, Inc.,
Publishers, and distributed in Canada by Word
Communications, Ltd., Richmond, British Columbia.

The Bible version used in this publication is THE NEW KING
JAMES VERSION. Copyright 1979, 1980, 1982, Thomas Nelson,
Inc., Publishers.

ISBN 0-7852-8195-9

Printed in the United States of America

1 2 3 4 5 6 — 99 98 97 96 95 94

Amy's Angel

Mary Manz Simon
Illustrated by Toni Wall

A
JANET
THOMA
BOOK

THOMAS NELSON PUBLISHERS
Nashville • Atlanta • London • Vancouver

4

One spring day Amy was trying to do
wheelies on her bike, just like her big sister.

Screeeeeccchh! The tires squealed.
Crrruuunch! Amy's bike scraped against the sidewalk.

6

Mom ran out of the house when she heard the noise.
"Ow! Ow! Mommy, it hurts. My chin really hurts," cried Amy.

Mom stooped down beside Amy. "Anything else hurt?" she asked. "No," replied Amy. "Just my chin. It hurts. It really hurts."

Mom looked closely at Amy's chin, then helped
her walk into the house. "Sit here by Grandma
while I call Dr. Gregory," she told Amy.

Amy sobbed softly. Her arm brushed
against Grandma's gold angel pin.

Soon Mom returned. "Dr. Gregory wants to look at that cut on your chin," Mom explained. "He'll meet us at the hospital."

"No, no," Amy cried. "I don't want to go. I don't want a shot."

12

Grandma put her arms around Amy. "I know how you feel, Honey." She took the angel pin off her dress. "Here, take my

angel pin," she said. "It will remind you that Jesus' angels are
with you wherever you go. And I'll be praying for you too."

Mom drove the car as Amy rested her head against the headrest. She watched the cars whiz past. Her chin hurt. Her eyes were filled with tears. She could hardly talk.

"We'll get there as soon as possible," Mom said.

Amy closed her eyes. A single tear rolled down her cheek.

There were so many lights in the hospital.
There were so many people in the hospital.
There were so many sounds in the hospital.
And everybody whispered.

"Hi, Amy," Dr. Gregory said as he came into the waiting room. "I hear your bike got all tangled up with your chin." Amy looked up. "I don't want a shot," she said loudly. "Well, let's just take a good look first."

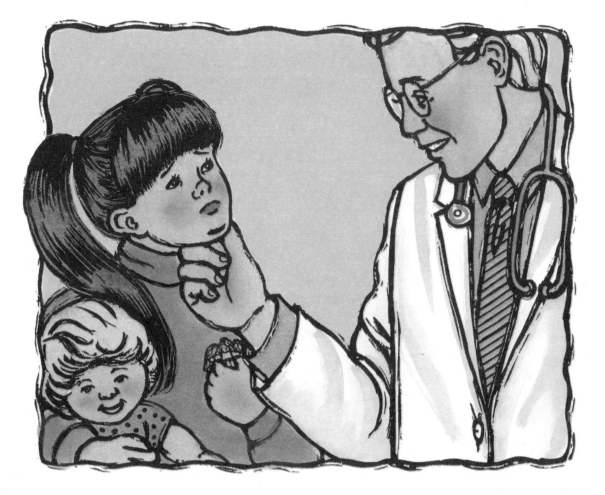

Dr. Gregory turned Amy's chin this way. Then he turned it that way. Finally he said, "We could put in a stitch. But I think a special bandage called a butterfly will work out fine."

"Oh, that's wonderful," said Mom.

Amy touched her angel pin.

Amy sniffed quietly. She walked through the door slowly. She turned to look at Mom one last time. "Dear Jesus, please send me an angel," she whispered as she touched Grandma's angel pin.

Less than a half hour later Amy and her mom were walking out of the hospital.

Amy didn't talk. Amy didn't cry. Amy just touched Grandma's angel pin. Yes, it was still there. And yes, the angel had been with her.

The butterfly felt tight on her chin, but the cut didn't hurt so much. It was all over now.

Grandma was waiting for Amy and Mom when they got home. She had baked Amy a surprise cake. "How did it go?" she asked.

"I didn't get a shot," Amy answered. "This is a butterfly." She pointed to her chin. "My chin still hurts, but not so bad."

"And my angel?" asked Grandma. "Did my angel pin remind you of Jesus' angels?"

Amy nodded. Then she asked, "Can the angel pin keep me from falling off my bike again?"